Winnie *at Her Best*

Winnie
at Her Best

by Jennifer Richard Jacobson

illustrated by Alissa Imre Geis

Houghton Mifflin Company
Boston 2006

Thanks to Keifer Schulz and his classmates at the Petingill School for helping me to write this story's ending, and to Sara Richard for her talk about the nature of a person's bones (thus sparking the idea for this book). Heartfelt thanks, also, to my editor, Ann Rider, and my marketing pal, Lisa DiSarro, who make me feel so very lucky to be a Houghton author.

Text copyright © 2006 by Jennifer Richard Jacobson
Illustrations copyright © 2006 by Alissa Imre Geis

www.houghtonmifflinbooks.com

The text of this book is set in 13-point Utopia.
The illustrations are graphite and caran d'ache crayon on bristol.

Library of Congress Cataloging-in-Publication Data
Jacobson, Jennifer, 1958–
Winnie at her best / by Jennifer Richard Jacobson ; illustrated by Alissa Imre Geis.
p. cm.
Summary: Zoe is the smartest speller and Vanessa is the top actress in
the fourth grade, but Winnie doesn't know what she does best.
ISBN 0-618-47277-0 (hardcover)
[1. Friendship—Fiction. 2. Self-realization—Fiction. 3. Reading—Fiction.]
I. Geis, Alissa Imre, ill. II. Title.
PZ7.J1529Wh 2005
[Fic]—dc22   2004026549

ISBN-13: 978-0618-47277-2

Manufactured in the United States of America
QUM 10 9 8 7 6 5 4 3 2 1

For Kelly and Sara—the best!
And to my third grade teacher, Mrs. Shepard,
who inspired a lifelong love of learning.
—J.R.J.

For Ann.
—A.I.G.

Chapter 1

"Winifred?"

The room was silent except for the sound of her teacher's voice.

"Could you repeat the word?" asked Winnie.

Several students groaned. Loudly. Winnie had already taken forever to think about this word.

"Cheer," said Mrs. Shepard. "The word is *cheer.*"

A simple word. A short word. Winnie knew she ought to be able to get *this* word right. But trying to think of the correct spelling during a spelling bee was hard. If Winnie were sitting at her desk, not standing in the front of the room, she would try to write the word.

Was it c-h-e-e-r? Or c-h-e-a-r? She could never

remember which words had *ee* and which had *ea*. She closed her eyes and tried to picture the commercial for the laundry detergent with the same name.

"Cheer," said Winnie. "C-h-e" — Winnie paused— "a-r?" Vanessa, one of Winnie's best friends, gasped. "Cheer."

"Incorrect," said Mrs. Shepard. Winnie left the line of spellers and sat down in her seat.

"Cynthia, spell *cheer*."

Well, of course Cynthia would spell it correctly. It was easy after someone had given the wrong spelling. How many ways were there to spell the word *cheer* anyway? Only two. And I, Winnie Fletcher, chose the wrong one, she thought.

"Zoe, the word is *margarine*. Spell *margarine*."

Margarine. Wow! That was a tough word. Winnie sat up straighter.

"Margarine. M-a-r," said Zoe.

You can do it, Zo, thought Winnie. Zoe was Winnie's other best friend. The three girls had been friends since kindergarten.

"G-a-r—" Winnie closed her eyes and tried to picture the spelling on the front of the margarine container at home. She couldn't see the letters, only a hand holding a slice of buttered bread. Winnie's stomach began to growl.

"I-n-e," said Zoe. "Margarine."

"Correct," said Mrs. Shepard.

Winnie smiled at Zoe. Then she looked at Vanessa, who was still standing. Vanessa raised her eyebrows as if to say, this is getting scary.

And sure enough, Vanessa's next word was a fright.

"Could you repeat the word?" asked Vanessa.

"Mountainous," said Mrs. Shepard. "The scenery was mountainous."

"Mountainous. M-o-u-n-t-a-n-o-u-s," said Vanessa. "Mountainous."

Winnie looked at Zoe. Zoe shook her head.

"Incorrect," said Mrs. Shepard. Vanessa shrugged and sat down.

There were four kids standing in the front of the room. Then three. Then Zoe and Cynthia.

"Cynthia, spell *persnickety*."

"Could you use it in a sentence, please?" asked Cynthia.

"The persnickety teacher insisted on neat handwriting."

Cynthia looked up as if she could see the spelling of the word in the air just above the students' heads. She listed the letters slowly and carefully.

"Incorrect," said Mrs. Shepard.

Cynthia bit her lip and started to sit down.

"Wait," said Mrs. Shepard. "If Zoe does not spell the word correctly, you both get another turn.

"Zoe, the word is *persnickety*."

Winnie and most of the other students held their breath.

"Persnickety. P-e-r-s-n-i-c-k-e-t-y," said Zoe. "Persnickety."

"That's correct," said Mrs. Shepard. "Zoe Johnson will represent our class in the school spelling bee. And if she wins that," Mrs. Shepard said, beaming, "she will go on to the city spelling championships."

Everyone in the class clapped. Winnie and Vanessa clapped the loudest.

"It's easy to spell the word when someone has spelled it wrong," whispered Cynthia.

Poor sport, thought Winnie.

Chapter 2

Walking home that afternoon, Winnie and Vanessa linked arms and sang their celebratory song.

Zoe's not small,
She's so tall,
She can carry the spelling bee on her back.
And when she walks it will shake,
And if she drops it, it will break!
Zoe's not small,
She's so tall,
She can carry the spelling bee on her back!

"I could never spell *persnickety*," said Winnie. Zoe bent to tie her sneaker. "You know," she

said, "Cynthia's really smart. Maybe she would have won the spelling bee if I had tried to spell the word first."

"Not true," said Vanessa, running in front of Zoe and then turning to bow down to her. "You,

O Spelling Bee Champion, are the smartest girl in fourth grade."

"And you are the best actress," said Zoe.

Winnie laughed. It was true. Vanessa was a born actress. The high school was putting on a performance of *The Sound of Music* this fall, and the director had invited fourth graders to audition for the parts of the Von Trapp kids. Vanessa was the only one from their school who got a part in the play.

"Zoe's the smartest," said Vanessa, "I'm the best actress, and you, Winifred Fletcher," she said, turning to Winnie, "you are the best—"

Winnie waited to hear what Vanessa would say. It seemed as if Vanessa had to check every cupboard in her brain to find an answer.

"You are the best—"

Winnie turned away, tripped over a crack in the sidewalk, and caught herself with her hands. For a moment she looked as if she were attempting a pushup on Clementine Street. She lowered herself to the ground.

"You are the best tumbler!" said Vanessa.

"Great," said Winnie as she sat up and pulled little pebbles out of her palms. "You mean stumbler."

"Oh, Winnie," said Zoe, helping her up. "You're good at lots of things."

"Name one," said Winnie.

"Drawing!" said Vanessa. "No one can draw as well as you."

"You don't know that," said Winnie. They were nearly at Winnie and Vanessa's house, and Winnie began to slow down. "A lot of kids can draw. Have you ever seen Henry's birds? Or Gracie's cartoons?"

"But we like *your* drawings," said Zoe.

"That's because you're my best friends," said Winnie.

"Marissa! What are you doing?" yelled Vanessa.

Winnie looked over at their house. Winnie and her dad lived on the first floor of the house. Vanessa, her sister, Marissa, and their parents lived on the second and third floors. Marissa was sitting on the front porch with a boy who looked like another kindergartner. He had hair that hung over his eyes and a shirt that practically went down to his knees.

"Me and John Stuart are making get-well tea," said Marissa, holding a handful of marigolds, roots and all.

"Mama's going to kill you when she sees how you've torn up her garden, Marissa Wiley."

"Stop bossing, Vanessa," said Marissa.

Winnie looked down and saw a mixture of dried leaves and twigs floating in a soup pot. "Who's sick?" she asked.

"None of your beeswax!" said the boy as he jumped up and raced down the street.

Winnie wanted to call out something, but she didn't know what to say.

"Boy, can he run!" said Zoe.

"Yup," said Marissa. "He's the best runner in kindergarten."

That night, Winnie pulled out all the drawings she had done since she was two years old from the bottom drawer of a bureau in their living room.

"What are you looking for, Win?" asked Mr. Fletcher, who was grading his students' papers nearby.

"Nothing," said Winnie. She looked at the first pictures she had drawn. There were pictures of people with legs coming out of their heads! And more advanced pictures of people with round bellies and big fat belly buttons. She found a picture of a horse, which looked more like a big dog, and the self-portrait that she had taken to camp last summer.

"Dad, how do you know if you're good at something? I mean really good at something and not just, well, ordinary?"

"That's a tough one, Win."

"Are you a good teacher?" asked Winnie.

Mr. Fletcher put down his pen. "Yes," he said. "Yes, I am a good teacher."

"But how do you know?"

"My students tell me."

"Are you the *best* teacher?"

"I wouldn't go that far," said Mr. Fletcher.

"Could you be the best at something if you wanted to be?" asked Winnie.

"Sure, but to be the best, you have to work very hard at it."

Winnie put all her drawings back into the drawer where her father kept them. That was it, Winnie thought. If she wanted to be special, like Zoe and Vanessa, she was going to have to work much harder at it.

Chapter 3

Before breakfast, before her father had even appeared for his morning coffee, Winnie was at the kitchen table drawing in her sketchbook. She had arranged a group of objects on the table to make a "still life." Her father had told her this artistic term when they had last visited the Museum of Fine Arts in Boston.

Winnie's arrangement included a ketchup bottle, a teddy bear mug she had had since she was a baby, and a dead fly. The fly was definitely the hardest thing Winnie had ever tried to draw.

Using the side of her pencil, Winnie made light lines to show where each object would go. Then, when she thought she had the placements right, she focused on one object at a time, trying to capture all its details. But it was hard. The ketchup bottle looked wiggly and the fly looked as if it were alive, flying upside down. Eventually Winnie had more eraser marks than pencil lines. She tore the drawing from her sketchbook and tossed it away.

"How come you're so grumpy?" Vanessa asked Winnie as the girls walked to school.

Winnie didn't know what to say. She didn't want to tell her friends about her picture. What would they care anyway? It wasn't like the picture was homework or anything. "A dead fly," said Winnie.

"A dead fly?" said Zoe.

The three girls looked at each other and laughed. But Winnie's mood didn't change until Mrs. Shepard announced that they would do something new in school today. "New" usually meant fun, at least for a while.

"You are going to be reading buddies," said Mrs. Shepard. "Once a week we will visit Mr. Mackie's kindergarten class. Each of you will be assigned a reading partner whom you will read to. Later, your kindergartner will read to you!"

"What should we read?" someone asked.

"That will be up to you," said Mrs. Shepard. "Though you'll want to choose a picture book for your first time together."

Mrs. Shepard walked the class down to the school library so they could choose their books. When they walked through the library door, kids ran to the shelves to pull off their favorite picture books.

"Wait," called Mrs. Shepard, not loudly, but in a voice that made everyone stop in his or her tracks. "Let me pass out the names of your students first. Then you can look for a book."

Winnie waited patiently as Mrs. Shepard handed out slips of paper. She knew that *Lilly's Purple Plastic Purse* would be gone. So would *Bootsie Barker Bites.* Finally she was handed a slip. She looked down at the name: John Stuart Godowsky. Where had she heard that name before?

Zoe looked over Winnie's shoulder. "You have the runner," she said.

"The runner?" asked Winnie.

"Yeah, the best runner in kindergarten," said Vanessa, joining them.

"Oh, yeah," said Winnie, smiling. The one who was making the get-well tea with Marissa. Then Winnie knew. She knew exactly which book she would choose to read to John Stuart Godowsky, whether it was any of her beeswax or not.

Chapter 4

Winnie entered the kindergarten class with the book *How Do Dinosaurs Get Well Soon?* under her arm. While the kindergarten teacher introduced kids to their reading buddies, Winnie searched for John Stuart, but he didn't seem to be there. Maybe *he's* the one who isn't feeling well, thought Winnie.

Winnie looked around the room, fondly. She remembered when she was in kindergarten and got to build with blocks or play in the house corner. Winnie noticed a classroom pet in a cage and moved out of the crowd to take a closer look—and that's when she spotted John Stuart. He wasn't in line waiting to meet his fourth-grade helper; he was hiding under the science table. Winnie knocked on the tabletop and crouched down.

"May I come in?" she asked.

John Stuart shrugged.

She took that as a yes and crawled under the table, too.

"Remember me?" asked Winnie. "I live in the same house as Marissa."

Again John Stuart shrugged.

"Want to listen to this book?" asked Winnie. She showed him the cover.

John Stuart played with the laces on one of his sneakers.

Winnie looked up. Vanessa was reading to a little girl who had snuggled so close to her, the reading buddies looked like sisters. The little girl lifted her eyes from the page and stared up at Vanessa. Vanessa stopped reading for a moment and smiled.

Zoe was reading a book about volcanoes to a little boy who was pointing to the pages. Every time Zoe began to read the words, the little boy would shout out questions: "What's this?" "Is this lava?" "How hot is lava?" "Does it burn you?"

Zoe caught Winnie's eyes and smiled a can-you-believe-this smile. Winnie smiled back. At least Zoe's reading buddy was interested.

Winnie looked over at John Stuart, who hadn't uttered a sound. "Well," she said. "I'm supposed to read to you, so I might as well get started." She scooted closer to him so he could see the pictures.

The dinosaur book was pretty silly, but the best kind of silly, the kind that makes you giggle. Only John Stuart wasn't giggling at all. He wasn't even smiling.

The boy's sour face made Winnie read faster. She didn't even stop to look at the pictures. When she got to the end of the book and slammed the cover shut, John Stuart said three words.

"Read it again."

Chapter 5

It was Wednesday. Normally Winnie, Vanessa, and
Zoe would go to the library after school. But today
was different. Zoe was staying after so Mrs. Shepard
could help her practice for the school spelling bee.
And Vanessa had play rehearsal, so Winnie joined
the afterschool walkers without them.

When Winnie and her friends went to the library,
they always did the same things in the same
order. First they jumped up the library steps two
at a time. The first girl to reach the top pushed
the button so the library doors would open auto-
matically. Inside, they would place last week's
books in the return slot. Then Winnie would stop
to read the bulletin board.

Vanessa and Zoe could never understand why Winnie liked reading posters that announced adult book groups, guitar lessons, or the need for a nanny, so they usually went into the library ahead of her.

To Winnie, the notes on the bulletin board were like secret messages—messages that could change a person's whole life. What if, after reading a notice, a woman went to a book-club meeting for the first time and there was the boy she had been in love with in the fourth grade? (Not that Winnie was in love with anyone, mind you.) Or what if the woman who offered to be a nanny was someone magical, like Mary Poppins? And maybe the person who took the guitar lessons would become the star of a famous rock band all because she had decided to read the bulletin board on a particular day.

Today, thought Winnie after jumping up the steps and being the one to push the automatic door opener, there will be a message for me.

She stood in front of the board. Her eyes traveled over a notice about a blood drive, an invitation to come to a toddlers' story hour, and a handwritten note from a person looking for an apartment. And then, sure enough, there was the type of announcement that Winnie longed for. The art museum was having a children's drawing contest. The first-place winner would receive art lessons and a free pass to the museum for a year!

Winnie took a notebook out of her backpack and carefully recorded the contest rules.

- Children ages 7–11 are eligible to enter
- Artwork must be original—no imitations of famous works will be accepted
- Deadline for all submissions is October 15

The deadline is in two weeks, thought Winnie. I'll have to really work hard to be the best artist in two weeks.

Then, instead of going to the children's room as she would normally do, she sat down at one of the big wooden tables in the adult room. She immediately felt more grown-up and serious. Pulling the notebook out of her backpack again, she looked around for something to sketch.

A woman had fallen asleep in one of the easy chairs. Her face was lined but peaceful. Her hand rested on an open book on her lap. Winnie decided to draw the woman's hand.

As she put her pencil to the paper, she could hear the sounds of the library: a woman asking for a library card, a man coughing, the sound of someone typing on a computer keyboard. But soon the sounds fell away, and it seemed as if there was nothing else in the room but the dozing woman, Winnie, and her pencil and paper. Winnie looked up from time to time to stare at the curve in the hand, but mainly she let her pencil lead her. If she didn't try to think too hard, she could *feel* the way her pencil line should move—she knew just where to turn the pencil on its side or where to pause and place more lines to create wrinkles. A thumb and three fingers began to emerge on the page.

"What are you doing?"

Winnie jumped. She turned to see Vanessa standing beside her.

"Nothing," said Winnie, closing her notebook. "What are you doing here? I thought you had play rehearsal."

"They only needed me for a half-hour," said Vanessa, "so I decided to come find you. Have you gotten your books yet?"

Winnie shook her head. She stood and followed Vanessa downstairs to the children's room, glancing back at the woman one last time. In the children's room, she went directly to the mysteries and searched for one she hadn't read. There were two books with NEW stickers on their spines. As Winnie pulled them off the shelf, she turned to look at the librarian, who was smiling at her.

When she was certain that Vanessa was lost in her own search, Winnie moved from the mystery section to the art section. She didn't know why she was being secretive. Why shouldn't she tell her best friends that she was going to enter an art contest? But something was stopping her.

There was, of course, the chance that she wouldn't win. That she'd discover there were many children in the city who were far more talented than she was. Vanessa and Zoe would be very kind. They would tell her that the judges had been wrong, that her art was wonderful, and that they thought she was the best artist of all. And in some ways that ending seemed worse than simply not telling them.

Winnie pulled out a book for young artists.

"What's that?" asked Vanessa, coming around the corner.

"Oh, just something I want to look at," said Winnie.

Vanessa glanced at the cover. "Are you checking it out?"

Trying to look as though she wasn't sure if it was something she wanted, Winnie flipped through the pages. "Yeah, I think I will," she said in a voice that she hoped sounded humdy-dum.

"I knew it!" said Vanessa.

"What?" asked Winnie. Had Vanessa seen the notice about the art contest, too?

"You *can* take out three books at a time. My mother thought we could only take two."

Chapter 6

John Stuart, Winnie noticed, seemed to love books and hate them at the same time. He loved *How Do Dinosaurs Get Well Soon?*, and he made Winnie promise that she'd bring it every time she came to his classroom. But he scowled when Winnie suggested that he try reading one of the little books that the kindergarten teacher passed around.

"Look, John Stuart, here's a book about a cat."

John Stuart didn't say anything.

Winnie sat as close to John Stuart as she dared, opened the book, and began reading:

The fat cat sat on the mat.
The fat cat sat on the hat.
The fat cat sat on the rat.

"Well," said Winnie. "It *isn't* very interesting. But look, you can read it, John Stuart! All you have to do is sound out the first letter of each new word."

John Stuart pointed to one word in the book. "Sat, sat, sat," he read three times.

Weird, thought Winnie.

That night, Winnie told her father about John Stuart. She was drawing at her dining room table. Her library book was open, and she was following the instructions for shading objects. She knew that if she added gray shadows to her picture of a can of tuna, it would look more real.

"Maybe he's just shy," said Mr. Fletcher as he scrubbed a pot. It was his turn to wash the dishes.

"Not shy, Dad," said Winnie. "Strange. Of all the kids in kindergarten, I had to get the strangest one."

"Does he imagine that his fingers are friendly little caterpillars that talk?"

"I was only four when I did that!" cried Winnie.

"Does his father walk like a penguin?" Mr. Fletcher did his famous walk around the kitchen.

"Dad!"

Mr. Fletcher smiled. "Do you remember how you learned to read, Win?"

Winnie tried to think back. "I sounded out words," she said.

"No, before that. Before you knew the sounds of all the letters."

"We played book tag!" Winnie remembered her dad writing a letter in the sand. She had to think of a book that began with that particular letter and then run! John Stuart loved to run. But she couldn't very well play *that* game in the classroom. Besides, it wasn't her job to teach him to read.

But the idea didn't go away entirely. Winnie thought about John Stuart reading "sat, sat, sat" and thought, Of course! He could read *sat* because he knows the sound of *s. S* is the first letter of *Stuart.*

Winnie looked down at her drawing and realized that with very little thinking, she had added a big fat cat sitting on the tuna can.

Chapter 7

The whole school filled the gym of Pettingil Elementary to watch the winners of each classroom spelling bee compete. For a moment, Winnie and Vanessa thought Zoe was going to miss the word *silhouette.* She paused and asked the principal to repeat it. Then she asked her to use the word in a sentence. But after thinking carefully (Winnie could always tell when Zoe was thinking by the way she raised her eyebrows), she spelled it correctly. Zoe won the school spelling bee. Now she would go on to compete in the city spelling bee!

The next morning, two high school kids came to Pettingil to interview Zoe for their school newspaper. Mrs. Shepard allowed everyone in the class to gather round.

"Do you get nervous?" asked the girl in cowboy boots.

"I try not to," said Zoe, "because then I can't think clearly."

"How can you stop from feeling nervous?" the boy with a notepad and pen asked.

"I try to forget that I'm in a gym in front of people. I pretend I'm just walking down the street, figuring out the spelling of a word."

Winnie remembered a time when Zoe walked up and down the sidewalk thinking of every word she could that ended in *tion: vacation, location, trepidation.* She smiled.

"Zoe loves thinking about words," said Vanessa.

The boy looked down at Vanessa. He squinted his eyes like he was trying to bring her into focus. "Hey," he said. "You're the girl who's acting in *The Sound of Music*!"

"That's right!" said the girl with the boots. "I

heard you at rehearsal. You have a great voice! Can we interview you after we talk to Zoe?"

"Certainly," said Vanessa in her movie-star voice.

Winnie knew that she should feel happy for her friends. They were both going to be in the high school newspaper, and they were only in fourth grade! Yet she couldn't help feeling...prickly. At recess, when Zoe and Vanessa were still inside talking to the older kids, Winnie made a list of all the reasons she was mad. No, not *mad*. Furious!

1. Vanessa always tries to get attention
2. Zoe pretends she's not the smartest kid in the fourth grade even though everyone knows she is
3. Vanessa's a great singer because she has a BIG mouth
4. Being the best at something like spelling is stupid

Winnie read her list and felt a knot grow to the size of a rock in her stomach. She tore the list out of her notebook, ran over to the trash can on the playground, and shredded it into tiny bits.

If her fingers were caterpillars that talked, they'd tell her that she, Winifred Fletcher, was a terrible friend.

That afternoon, Winnie called Vanessa's mom and asked if it was okay if she came home right after school.

"Of course you can, sweetie," said Mrs. Wiley. "I'll be right here if you need anything."

Winnie told Vanessa and Zoe that she didn't feel good and walked home alone. It wasn't a lie really. She did feel crummy, and there was only one thing that she could do to make herself feel better. She would win that art contest.

Chapter 8

Winnie had no idea what to draw for the contest. She looked around her room for inspiration. Sea glass? Too small. Her recently started snow globe collection? No, drawing those miniature snowy worlds would drive her crazy. There was the teddy bear she'd had since she was two. His fur was matted and all the color on his eyes had worn off. But she bet that lots of kids would draw their teddy bears. Winnie wanted her picture to look different.

Eventually, she did what she always did when she was out of ideas. She pulled out two photo albums from beneath her bed. The first was an album that her father had given her. Inside were pictures of Winnie's mom, who had died soon after Winnie was born. She liked to stare at the pictures and imagine what it would be like to know this smiling woman who had been her mother. "Any ideas, Mom?" she said.

Winnie flipped through the second book, which contained pictures from Winnie's life. On the next to last page was a picture her dad had taken last summer. The picture made her feel happy, but it also reminded her of the list she had written during recess, and that made her feel sad. She pulled the picture from the album, found a real artist's pencil that her third-grade teacher had given her, scooped up her sketchbook, and stretched out on the living room floor to draw.

She had just finished creating the outline of her picture when she heard a *thump, thump, thump* on the porch. It sounded like Marissa jumping up and down on the front steps. If Marissa was home, Vanessa probably was too. Winnie decided to take a break and see.

But it was John Stuart, not Marissa, who was making all the noise. He looked up at Winnie peering through the door, then turned and ran.

"Wait! Stop!" yelled Winnie, running after John Stuart. She saw him run up the steps and into his yellow house—the very house that made everyone ask, "When are they going to paint that thing?" when walking by.

Winnie stood on the sidewalk. She glanced up at the house and saw John Stuart's face in the front window.

Why did he run away? Did he think she would be mad at him for making noise? Winnie walked up the steps and rang the doorbell.

"Would you like to play a game, John Stuart?" she asked when he opened the door just a crack.

"I'm watching *Mr. Marshmallow* on TV."

"This game's really fun," said Winnie. "I used to play it when I was your age. We could play in your backyard."

John Stuart shrugged.

"Who is it, John Stuart?" John Stuart's mother came to the porch.

"My reading buddy," said John Stuart.

"Why, Winnie, it's nice to meet you! Come in," said Mrs. Godowsky. She had a friendly face, but she looked cold. She carried a blanket around her shoulders.

Mrs. Godowsky turned off the TV and told Winnie to sit down for a moment.

"I thought John Stuart might like to come out and play a game," said Winnie.

"Oh. That's a lovely idea! With my tired bones, John Stuart doesn't get much opportunity to play the way he should."

John Stuart jumped up. "You don't have tired bones!" he said. "You have happy bones."

It was the most words Winnie had ever heard John Stuart say.

Mrs. Godowsky smiled. "You know what would make these happy bones even happier?"

"What?" asked John Stuart.

"If you would go outside and have fun with Winnie."

John Stuart didn't say anything else. He simply led Winnie to the backyard.

Winnie drew a box in a patch of dirt and explained the rules to John Stuart. Then she wrote the letter *H* inside the box.

"Tell me the name of a book that begins with this letter," said Winnie.

John Stuart just stared.

"It's an *H*," said Winnie. "You know, the letter that says ha-ha."

"How Do Dinosaurs Get Well Soon?!" said John Stuart, and he took off running. He ran around the house and under a rusty swing set. It took Winnie a long time to catch him.

"Your turn," she said.

John Stuart just stood there. He didn't even look up at Winnie.

"Think of a title and put the first letter in the box."

John Stuart still didn't move.

"Okay, I'll do another one." Winnie put a *C* in the box.

"I don't know any books," said John Stuart.

Winnie was going to say, "What do you mean you don't know any books?" but then she got an idea. She wrote an *M* in the box. "This is a TV show," she said.

John Stuart looked up at Winnie.

"It's an *M*," said Winnie. "*M* says *mmmmmm*."

"It does?" John Stuart looked amazed. His eyes grew bright. *"Mr. Marshmallow!"* he yelled, and took off running again.

"I thought you weren't feeling well," said Vanessa. She was sitting on their front porch when Winnie returned from John Stuart's house.

"I wasn't," said Winnie.

"But now you're okay?"

"Yeah. I guess so," said Winnie. "What did those high school kids ask you?"

"They asked me if I had ever taken acting lessons and which aspect did I like more, the acting or the singing."

"What did you say?"

Vanessa put one hand behind her head as if she were posing for a glamorous photograph. "I said, 'That's enough questions for now. Please contact my agent.'"

"You did not!" shouted Winnie.

Vanessa laughed. "Remember when you and

Zoe and I used to sit behind the school at recess and pretend we were famous?"

"You pretended your phone never stopped ringing!" said Winnie.

"And you pretended you had adopted a million kids," said Vanessa.

"And that I lived in a mansion on wheels!"

"Wouldn't it be fun if we could still make those things up?" asked Vanessa.

"Let's put them in a story!" said Winnie. "You and Zoe and I could write about them at recess."

"It's a plan," Vanessa said just as Mr. Fletcher called Winnie to set the table.

Chapter 9

Winnie stood patiently in line waiting to use the pencil sharpener. She didn't mind that Cynthia was taking so long, because she had two great things to think about.

Last night, her dad had offered to take her drawing and have it framed before they dropped it off for judging at the art museum. He even called someone who worked at the museum and learned that five top entries would be chosen for the final judging at the children's art festival. Winnie would know ahead of time if she had made it to the top five.

And at recess, she would write zany stories with Vanessa and Zoe. It seemed as if they never had time to just play around anymore. Maybe I will be the best artist *and* the best writer when I grow up, she thought.

"Winnie," said Mrs. Shepard. "Would you come see me for a moment?"

Winnie stepped out of line with her broken pencil and went up to her teacher's desk.

"I have an e-mail here from Mr. Mackie, the kindergarten teacher. Apparently he talked with both John Stuart and his mother. They're thrilled that you're helping John Stuart learn to read."

Winnie smiled. She couldn't believe that her teacher had learned of their game of book tag.

"Mr. Mackie was wondering if you would be able to come down to the kindergarten classroom during our recess today to help John Stuart some more. Apparently what you're doing is working and he doesn't want it to stop."

"I was going to write stories with Vanessa and Zoe at recess," said Winnie.

"Oh, dear," said Mrs. Shepard. "I told Mr. Mackie

that I was sure you'd be delighted. Of course, I should have checked with you first."

"Well," said Winnie.

"What you're doing is a wonderful thing," said Mrs. Shepard.

Then why doesn't it feel like a wonderful thing? thought Winnie. Why does this feel like a punishment? But she nodded just the same.

At recess time Zoe and Vanessa waved as Winnie walked down the kindergarten hallway.

"How can we play book tag in here?" asked John Stuart in a loud voice. He seemed just as surprised to see Winnie in his classroom as she was to be there.

Winnie looked around the cramped room. Kindergarten children were writing, drawing, and gluing at tables. They were building with pattern blocks and puzzles on the floor. Children in plastic smocks were painting at side-by-side easels.

John Stuart was right. There was no way that they could play tag in here.

"I know," said Winnie. "Let's get some paper and go to the book corner. We'll take turns writing letters on a piece of paper and finding books that begin with that letter."

They made piles of books that began with the letters *A, B, C, D,* and *E.* John Stuart looked up at the letters on the wall and wrote an *F.*

Winnie looked through the books. She found one called *Fox in Socks* and another titled *Fire on the Mountain.* Then she found a book with fathers on the front.

"I don't want that one," said John Stuart.

"Why?" asked Winnie. "*Fathers* begins with *F.*"

"But I don't have a father and I don't want it," said John Stuart.

Winnie paused. Then she put it back in a bin. "You know, John Stuart," she said, sitting down next to him on the rug, "I don't have a mother."

"You don't?" asked John Stuart. "What happened to her?"

"She died when I was a baby."

John Stuart wrinkled his forehead. "How come she died?"

"She was very sick," said Winnie.

John Stuart jumped up as if a bee had stung him.

"I don't want to read anymore!" he said.

"But, John Stuart," said Winnie.

"I'm done. Go back to your room now!" John Stuart shouted, and stomped to the other side of the classroom.

The class looked up at Winnie. Everyone was silent, waiting for her to respond. She didn't know what to do.

"I'm sorry, Winnie," said Mr. Mackie, coming over to her. "It seemed like such a good idea."

She tried to think of what she'd done wrong.

"I really appreciate your help," said Mr. Mackie.

Winnie nodded and, without looking up, raced out the door.

Later that night, Winnie felt like a mosquito looking for someone to bite. She had erased and erased and erased the same pair of eyes in her drawing.

"Maybe you should give it a rest," said Mr. Fletcher. He was correcting papers while Winnie

drew nearby. "Sometimes it helps to leave something alone for a little while."

"I can't leave it alone!" she said. "The deadline for the art contest is the day after tomorrow!"

"But if you ruin your drawing now," said Mr. Fletcher, "you won't have anything for the contest."

What her father said was true. Winnie closed her sketchbook and got ready for bed. This was definitely a day she wanted to forget.

Chapter 10

Fortunately, Winnie was rested enough to complete her drawing the next morning.

"Careful," Mr. Fletcher cautioned as Winnie erased one eye in the picture. "Perfection can be the enemy of art."

"There," said Winnie, making her changes and stepping back to look.

Mr. Fletcher put his arm around Winnie. "Wow! Winnie. You sure knew what you were doing. It looks wonderful."

Together Mr. Fletcher and Winnie walked to the framing shop. A friend of Mr. Fletcher's showed Winnie different colors of matt board and how they changed the feeling of her drawing. Orange made the drawing feel more zany, navy made it seem quieter. Winnie chose a matt that seemed to contain all the warmth of the sun.

After school, Mr. Fletcher and Winnie delivered the drawing to the art museum together.

"Ooh," said the woman who was in charge of the contest. That was all. Just "ooh."

There was a special room where contestants' pictures were being mounted. The woman at the museum pointed to the wall where Winnie's work would hang. There were lots of pictures of dogs, sneakers, and teddy bears—just as Winnie had suspected. Then Winnie saw a picture of a lighthouse that looked so real, she felt as if she could smell the salt air. Beside it was a picture of a horse that looked like it came from a picture book. Perhaps, thought Winnie, I won't be the best artist after all.

The next week was the slowest Winnie could ever remember. Zoe spent all her time with a tutor, preparing for the city spelling bee. Vanessa was involved in play rehearsals every single afternoon.

Both Winnie and Mr. Fletcher had forgotten to ask how the winners of the art contest would be notified, so every day Winnie checked the mail, the telephone messages, and her e-mail. When Mr. Fletcher met her in the afternoon, the first thing she asked him was, "Did you get a phone call or an e-mail?"

Each time, he shook his head.

When the opening night of *The Sound of Music* came, Winnie got permission to go with Vanessa's family—and Zoe—to watch. Never had Winnie stayed up so late on a school night. Mr. Fletcher said he would meet everyone at the school gymnasium.

Winnie could not take her eyes away from the stage, not even when her father arrived. She temporarily forgot that she was watching Vanessa. Instead she believed her friend was one of the Von Trapp family members—that she had a strict father, a wonderful nanny, and that she had to sneak out of Austria in a time of war.

No one clapped harder or hooted louder at the end than Winnie and Zoe.

After Winnie hugged Vanessa backstage, Mr. Fletcher pulled her aside. "Guess what I learned today?" he said.

Winnie didn't dare say anything. She studied her father's face for clues.

"Your drawing has been chosen as one of the top five in your age group!" said Mr. Fletcher.

"Yahoo!" shouted Winnie.

"What?" asked Vanessa and Zoe together.

Should she tell them? Was now the time?

"Yahoo for Vanessa," Winnie said. "You are definitely the best actress."

It was, after all, Vanessa's big night.

Chapter 11

The judging of the drawings for the children's art festival was to take place on a Saturday afternoon. Mr. Fletcher taught a college class in the morning, but he said that he would definitely meet Winnie at the museum.

"Are you sure you don't want Vanessa or Zoe to come along with you on the bus?" asked Mr. Fletcher as he handed her bus tokens.

Winnie thought for a moment. Though she had ridden the bus a gazillion times, she had never taken it all by herself. And it would be so much fun to tell them that her picture was chosen as one of the top five. She could imagine how happy her friends would be for her.

"You go ahead, Dad. I'll call them and see if they want to come." But first, thought Winnie, I'll have to tell them about the contest.

"Okey-doke, artichoke," said Mr. Fletcher, picking up his briefcase overflowing with papers. "I'll see you there."

Winnie waited for her father to leave and then she dialed Zoe's number.

"How's the studying going, Zo?" she asked.

"It's arduous," said Zoe. "A-r-d-u-o-u-s."

Winnie didn't know what *arduous* meant, but she knew that it didn't sound good. "Can you take a break this afternoon?" asked Winnie. "To do something really—"

Zoe interrupted. "I can't do *anything*, Winnie, except study. I've gotten this far and I don't want to let anyone down. I don't want to let myself down."

Winnie wished she could tell Zoe that she wouldn't let anyone down by not winning, but that would only make Zoe mad. What word did her father use when he wanted to say that something made the situation worse? "Exacerbate," said Winnie, remembering.

"Exacerbate," said Zoe. "E-x-a-c-e-r-b-a-t-e. Thanks, Win, I better go."

Winnie listened to the dial tone for a few moments after Zoe hung up, and then she dialed Vanessa's number.

Marissa answered. "How come John Stuart got mad at you at school?" she asked when she heard Winnie's voice.

"I don't know," said Winnie.

"He wouldn't play with me the rest of the day."

"I'm sorry," said Winnie. For what, she wasn't sure.

"My mom wants to know if you want to come up here and be with us," said Marissa.

Winnie thought for a moment. "No thanks," she said. "Tell your mom I have to leave for somewhere else soon."

"Okay," said Marissa and hung up. Winnie

never got to speak to Vanessa. But maybe that was okay. It didn't seem right to tell one best friend about the art contest before the other.

Suddenly the apartment seemed like a big cave isolated on a mountain. Winnie turned on the TV, but even Saturday morning cartoons felt long and boring. She fixed herself an early lunch—a peanut butter and banana sandwich. Then she practiced standing on her head, something she had promised herself she would be able to do by the end of fourth grade.

Finally, Winnie decided that it would not be too early to walk to the bus stop. She put on her favorite black velvet pants, her softest purple shirt, and the locket with her mother's picture inside. She opened the locket and stared at the photograph. "I'm going to the art museum now, Mom," she said, closed her eyes, and made a wish.

As Winnie fiddled with her front door for a few moments, making sure it had locked properly, she heard a screaming siren. She turned around and saw an ambulance, with lights flashing, racing down Clementine Street. The ambulance stopped right in front of John Stuart's house.

Chapter 12

Winnie rushed across the street. She was joined by other curious neighbors who all showed concern when Mrs. Godowsky was carried out on a stretcher. John Stuart's mother's eyes were shut, her face pale.

John Stuart was nowhere in sight. Winnie walked closer to the ambulance to see if he was sitting in the front.

"I can't get the boy to come out from under the bed," said one of the rescue workers.

"You may have to reach in and pull him out," said another.

Poor John Stuart, thought Winnie. She thought

of the time he had hidden under the science table. "Maybe I can talk to him," she said.

The two men didn't seem to hear her.

"I know John Stuart. I might be able to get him out," she said in a louder voice.

The two men looked at Winnie.

"Come on then," said one of them.

As Winnie climbed the stairs she called out, "John Stuart. John Stuart, it's me, Winnie."

John Stuart didn't wait for Winnie to come into his room. He dashed out and clung to her waist.

"What happened?" asked Winnie.

"My mother fell on the floor," he said. "And I called 911."

"Wow, you knew how to do that? You did the right thing!" said Winnie.

He began to cry. "Is she dead?"

"No, son," said the rescue worker. "But we need to get her to the hospital as quickly as possible. Would you like to come for a ride in the ambulance?"

"Only if Winnie comes," said John Stuart.

"I can't come," said Winnie. "But these rescuers will take good care of you, John Stuart."

"Winnie, no! You have to come!" John Stuart tightened his grip around Winnie.

"Officer Jennings has offered to drive the children. He'll be right behind us," the other man called from the bottom of the stairs.

Winnie wanted to say "I can't go," but she knew that the ambulance had to leave. She would talk to Officer Jennings herself.

Chapter 13

Winnie looked down at her watch. She needed to be at the museum in one hour. She took John Stuart's hand and led him outside. The policeman was waiting for them on the front steps.

"Officer Jennings," she said. "I am supposed to be somewhere else right now. My father's meeting me."

"That's okay," he said. "John Stuart, you can come with me."

"No, Winnie!" cried John Stuart. He grabbed her arm with both hands.

"There's nothing to be frightened of, John Stuart," she said. "You'll have fun riding in the police car."

John Stuart's eyes continued to beg her.

She crouched down. "John Stuart, I'm in a contest today. It's something I really want to do."

John Stuart's lip trembled.

Winnie's feet felt frozen in place. "I'll go," she said. After all, she thought, there must be a bus from the hospital to the museum.

When they entered the hospital, Officer Jennings told the man sitting at an enormous desk that they were looking for Mrs. Godowsky. He looked her name up on a computer and said he would get someone who could help them.

A nurse came down and explained to them that Mrs. Godowsky was with a doctor now, but that she was awake and eager to see her little boy. Officer Jennings said goodbye and the nurse brought them to a waiting room, where Winnie and John Stuart tried to watch a show on television.

Winnie looked at the clock on the wall. There was still a half-hour before the contest. "John Stuart," she said, scooting down in front of him, "I'm going to leave you here now and you can see your mom."

"No!" He jumped up. "You can't go!"

"Why? You'll get to see your mother. And the nurses will take good care of you."

"No, Winnie."

"That's not fair, John Stuart."

"Why?"

"Because maybe I'll be chosen as the best artist."

"But *why?*"

"Why what, John Stuart?" Winnie cried.

"Why do you have to *go?*"

Winnie tried to find words to tell John Stuart what she imagined would happen. How they would call her name and she would walk through a crowd of people to get her prize. A newspaper photographer would take her picture, and then the whole city would know that she had won this contest. Her dad would be so proud of her he wouldn't stop smiling. And on Monday, Vanessa and Zoe would cheer when her name was announced over the intercom at school.

"I just have to!" Winnie said, standing. "But I'll come back." She walked to the door of the room and turned to say goodbye.

John Stuart sat back down on the chair. Winnie knew that he was holding back tears. He was trying hard to be brave. "Bye, Winnie," he said.

"Bye," said Winnie, and she turned and walked down the hall. Her heart felt ten pounds heavier— too heavy to carry, too heavy to carry for one more step. She stopped. Should she leave?

Of course she should! There was the contest. She had worked so hard.

Then she thought of John Stuart sitting right

here, sitting all alone on the long train of chairs. She wanted to win the art contest in the worst way, but she wanted something else, too. She wanted to stay with John Stuart.

"You're right, John Stuart," said Winnie, walking back into the room.

John Stuart raised his head. His eyes brightened.

"I don't have to go," Winnie said. "But I do have to call my father and tell him where I am." She found the same nurse who had brought them to the waiting room. The nurse called the museum and talked to Mr. Fletcher.

Finally a doctor came into the room. "You must be John Stuart," she said. "Would you like to see your mom now?"

John Stuart jumped up and raced down the hall.

"Hold on!" shouted the doctor. "I'll show you where she is."

Winnie looked up at the clock. Had they begun to announce the winners? She tried not to think about it. She picked up a magazine with famous people in it and turned the pages, but none of the words made sense.

She got a better idea. She walked back to the nurses' station and asked for paper and a pencil. Then she lay down on the floor of the waiting room and began to draw. She sketched a bedroom with a bed, a bureau, and a rocking chair. Under the bed Winnie drew a little boy hiding.

"There you are!" said Mr. Fletcher, coming into the room.

Winnie jumped up and hugged her dad tight.

"It must not have been easy to give up your plans for today, Win," he said.

Chapter 14

The doctor returned to say that Mrs. Godowsky would love to talk to Winnie, and she invited Mr. Fletcher to come, too.

John Stuart was kneeling on the end of his mother's bed.

"Hi, Winnie," said Mrs. Godowsky, smiling.

"This is my father," said Winnie. "Ben Fletcher."

"Ben, I am so grateful to your—"

"Do you still have tired bones?" John Stuart interrupted.

Mrs. Godowsky laughed. "Yes, I suppose I do. But you have very brave bones!"

"Yes," said the doctor. "Was that you who called 911?"

John Stuart nodded.

"And was that *you* who put an aspirin under your mother's tongue when she fell?"

John Stuart looked worried—as if he didn't know if he had done a right thing or a wrong thing. "Mama said that aspirin would help her if she got really sick," he said quickly. "But there were two white bottles in the cupboard, and I didn't know which one was right."

"Well, you picked the right one," said the doctor.

"I read it," said John Stuart.

"You read it?" asked Mrs. Godowsky.

"Yes," said John Stuart. "I thought about the first sound of aspirin—*aaaa. A* for *aaaa.* Like *Alligator Sue* and *Apple Pie Fourth of July.* Aspirin starts with *a!*"

Winnie had had no idea that John Stuart remembered so much from their games.

"You not only have brave bones, you have smart bones!" said his mother, hugging him.

Mr. Fletcher said he would be more than happy to take care of John Stuart until Mrs. Godowsky's sister arrived from Iowa.

"Don't you worry, John Stuart," said the doctor. "We have a way to help your mother get better."

Winnie had seen John Stuart smile once or twice before, but never a smile as big as the one he was wearing now.

On the bus ride home, Winnie took out the drawing she had worked on at the hospital. She tucked that picture in the back of the pad and began a new sketch. This time she drew a picture of a boy jumping on a hospital bed. She knew that John Stuart hadn't really jumped on the bed, but she liked drawing him this way. His legs were bent high and his arms wide open. Mr. Fletcher looked down at her drawing and smiled.

"I have something for you," he whispered, shifting a sleeping John Stuart from one side of his lap to the other.

Winnie watched as her dad slowly pulled a red ribbon from his pocket.

Second place.

"Not bad," he said, beaming.

Winnie gave her dad a strained smile. She knew she should be happy. A red ribbon meant she had *almost* won first place. Almost was good, wasn't it?

But a little sad feeling crawled into the corner of Winnie's throat and held on tight.

She hadn't been at the art museum when the winners were called. She hadn't marched up and collected the ribbon herself. And she hadn't won first place.

Winnie kept her head down, staring at the red ribbon in her hand until they reached their stop.

Chapter 15

"Winnie, where were you?" asked Vanessa, slowing the wide swing of the jump rope. Zoe stopped jumping to watch as Mr. Fletcher, John Stuart, and Winnie walked down the street.

"John Stuart!" said Marissa, dropping her end of the rope. "What are you doing here?"

"My mother is in the hospital," said John Stuart.

"Winnie went with John Stuart to the hospital," said Mr. Fletcher, "instead of going to the art museum."

"That's too bad about your mom," Zoe said to John Stuart. "Will she be all right?"

John Stuart nodded. "The doctor said they can fix her."

Vanessa pointed to the ribbon Winnie held in her hand. "What's that?" she asked.

"I won second place in the city art contest."

"You did?" said Zoe. "Wow."

"It's too bad that she couldn't be there," said Mr. Fletcher.

"Well, now we know," said Vanessa.

"What?" asked Winnie.

"Zoe is the best speller, I am the best actress, and you, Winifred Fletcher, are one of the best—"

"Artists!" yelled John Stuart.

Vanessa and Zoe laughed.

So did Winnie.

"And, one of the best *friends*," said Vanessa.

"Yes!" said John Stuart.

"*The* best," said Zoe.

Winnie looked down at the ribbon in her hand and smiled. Winning second place seemed better now that she had told her friends about it.

Zoe chanted:

Winnie's not small,
She's so tall,
She can carry the art contest—

"And a friend," piped in Vanessa.

On her back!

And the next day, three best friends, one kindergarten friend, and one dad took a trip to the art museum.